To Joe, for our playful dinner
conversations that inspired this book,
to Pema, who gets me giggling,
and in loving memory of Trish,
who cooked so many a divine dish!

THE THANK YOU DISH?

by Trace Balla

Kane Miller
A DIVISION OF EDC PUBLISHING

It was dinnertime at Grace's place.

"Thanks to the rain, the soil and the sunshine," said Mama.

"And thank you, kangaroos," said Grace.

"Kangaroos?" said Mama.
"Why would you thank
the kangaroos?"

"Well, I'm thanking the kangaroos for not eating all the carrots," said Grace.

"Ah," said Mama.

"Well, I'm thanking Leo for lending me the ladder...

...so I could pick the lemons from lovely Lily's tree," said Grace.

"Ah," said Mama.

"And thank you, alpaca," said Grace.

"Alpaca?" asked Mama.
"Why would you thank
an alpaca?"

"Well, I'm thanking the alpaca for the wool, so that Auntie Amber could knit the scarf...

...that kept Uncle
Fred from freezing when
he caught the fish," said Grace.

"Ah," said Mama.

"And thank you, road workers," said Grace.

"Well, I'm thanking the road workers for fixing the path, so we could ride our bikes along the creek...

...all the way to Suki's stand to buy some corn and kale," said Grace.

"Ah," said Mama.

"Hey, I've got one too," said
Mama. "Thank you, flower tree."

"Flower tree?" said Grace.
"Why would you thank
the flower tree?"

"Well, I'm thanking the flower tree because that's how we met Trish, when you said that her dress matched the tree."

"Ah," said Grace.

"And," said Grace, "now that we're friends..."

...she's given us some of her homemade sauce!"

"I never knew there were so many thanks to give for just one dinner!" said Mama.

"Well, I've got one more," said Grace.

"Thank you, Mama."

"Me?" said Mama. "Why would
you thank me?"

"I'm thanking you for cooking such a yummy dinner,
of course!" said Grace.

"My pleasure," said Mama. "Thanks for saying thanks!"

About the author

Trace takes great delight in knowing where the food she eats comes from.
She can sometimes be spotted out foraging for food, or cycling around her neighborhood
of Castlemaine, central Victoria, with a basketful of homegrowns to share.
If you give a wave, she might even ring her bell!

Special thanks to Elise Jones, Ruth Grüner, Erica Wagner, Trudy White and Joe Flexmore.

First American Edition 2017
Kane Miller, A Division of EDC Publishing

Copyright © Trace Balla 2017

First published in Australia by Allen & Unwin in 2017

For information contact:
Kane Miller, A Division of EDC Publishing
PO Box 470663
Tulsa, OK 74147-0663
www.kanemiller.com
www.edcpub.com
www.usbornebooksandmore.com

Library of Congress Control Number: 2016956728

Printed in China
1 3 5 7 9 10 8 6 4 2

ISBN: 978-1-61067-644-1